To Buckets, my little angel.

You inspire me every day to be a better version of myself. I love you more than words can express. Your quirkiness, silliness, and inquisitive nature inspired this book. I hope others can see your true personality shine in these pages.

To Buckets's family, whom I couldn't have done this without. Your love and support of Buckets is evident every day. Michael, Ceasar, and Ana Castro, Lewis, Debbie, Bryan, Jennifer, Eli, Zac, and Cameron Crowder, and Carolina and Joe Ousley, thank you.

www.mascotbooks.com

Buckets Goes on a Winter Adventure

For more information, please contact:
Mascot Books
620 Herndon Parkway, Suite 320
Herndon, VA 20170
info@mascotbooks.com

Library of Congress Control Number: 2019903731

CPSIA Code: PRT0719A
ISBN-13: 978-1-64307-369-9

Printed in the United States

Buckets
Goes On a Winter Adventure

Taryn Crowder
Illustrated by Nidhom

Buckets has always been a curious pup.

For as long as he can remember, he felt different than other dogs.

He wonders about where things come from.

He wonders about things big and small.

Buckets likes to sit perched on his sofa, watching all that happens outside his window. During the winter, he likes to watch the snow fall.

He begins to wonder,
*Where does the snow
come from?*

On his walks, his
humans keep him
on a short leash, so
he's never able to
find out.

One day, his humans leave the front door cracked while they unload the car.

Buckets thinks, *This is my chance! I can sneak out and find where the snow comes from! I'll be quick. My humans won't even know I'm gone.*

Buckets sneaks out the front door and runs and runs.

He keeps thinking, *I'll run to where the snow starts and* **THEN** *I'll find where it comes from!*

He starts to get tired.
He's been running a long time.

He stops and looks around...he realizes
he has no idea where he is.

The snow...it's not stopping, he thinks.
I don't know where my house is.

He starts to get really cold. *This was a
bad idea. What do I do now?*

He sniffs the ground, hoping he'll be able to smell his way back, but the snow is covering his path and he can't smell which way is home.

Buckets realizes he just kept running, and didn't pay attention to where he was going. *Why did I do that?* he thinks. *My humans don't even know I left. What if they never find me or I never find them?*

Buckets starts to get sad. He doesn't know what to do.

Just when he starts to think he's lost
forever, a little red bird lands on his head.

"Hi, there," the bird says. "My name is
Rhea. I was watching you from up in my
nest, and you look lost. Is everything okay?"

"No. No…it's not. You see, I left my house to find out where the snow comes from and I ran and ran until I ended up here. I'm lost. And I definitely won't ever find where the snow comes from, or where my house is," Buckets says.

"I see," Rhea says. "Well, I've been alive for some time and have seen many things. I can help you find your home and I can tell you all about where the snow comes from."

"You…you…you can?!" says Buckets. "I'd be forever grateful. I'm Buckets, by the way. Where should we start?"

"I'll fly over you and navigate. I can still see your tracks from above. And, I'll tell you all about where the snow comes from."

Buckets has never been this happy. He is going to find his way home and learn where the snow comes from!

As Rhea and Buckets set off on their journey,
she starts telling him **allllll** about the snow.

"You see, I've flown all over. My ancestors were some of the first Northern Cardinals in existence. My kind don't migrate for winter, so we have seen a lot of snow."

Buckets listens intently from below. He can't believe he's so lucky to have gotten help from such a wise bird.

Rhea continues. "The snow comes from the mighty clouds, which rule the sky. Everything in the air must pass through the clouds. Snow forms when little bits of clouds go from being wet air to ice. Snow can only form in really cold clouds."

"Wowwww," Buckets says in amazement. "My favorite part about snow is watching the snowflakes fall!"

"Did you know that no two snowflakes are the same, just as no two dogs, birds, or people are the same?" Rhea asks. "We are all unique, and each and every one of us is beautiful in our own way."

Rhea goes on. "Every snowflake has six sides, but each snowflake falls and floats through the clouds with different temperatures and moisture levels, which shapes each snowflake in a unique way."

Buckets's face freezes with astonishment.

"I can't wait to get home and tell my humans everything I learned tonight!" Buckets exclaims.

"Speaking of home, it looks like we're here. Your tracks have stopped." Rhea says.

"This is it! This is home!
How will I ever repay you, Rhea?"

"Just remember to never
leave home alone without
letting your humans
know. I've been around
long enough to know that
they've been very worried
about you."

"Never again, Rhea. I've learned my lesson. Thank you, friend. I hope our paths cross again…when I'm safely walking with my humans," Buckets says, and giggles.

Buckets runs to his door and barks and barks.

His parents rush to the door and yell,
"BUCKETS! It's you!"

They pick him up and hug him tight, while Buckets shakes with excitement and licks their faces.

"Buckets, you can't ever do that to us again. We were so worried. We thought we'd lost you forever," they say.

His mom starts crying as she hugs him even tighter.

Buckets barks back, "I'll never leave you again. I'm so sorry…I love you."

With a lick and a grin, Buckets says, "I should have never left like that…but guess what? I learned about where snow comes from. Let me tell you all about it…"

About the Author

Taryn Crowder grew up in southern Virginia. After high school, she moved to Salem, Virginia, where she went to Roanoke College and majored in English literature with a concentration in communication studies. Upon graduation, she moved to Washington, D.C., where she spent five years working in marketing, PR, and event planning in a variety of industries. She now resides in San Diego, California, where she lives with her boyfriend and her dog, Buckets. Taryn has continued event planning, and started writing books. She has always been a dog lover: she grew up with three Labradors and, three years ago, she got her French Bulldog, Buckets, in San Diego. She regularly posts content to Buckets's Instagram account @nothingbut_buckets and creates Buckets-inspired products, which can be found at

www.bucketsthefrenchie.com.

About Buckets

Buckets is a blue pied French Bulldog, born and raised in San Diego, California. He has a big personality, and he is much more concerned with what humans are doing than what other dogs are doing. At the park, you can find him huddled around the humans, waiting for belly rubs and sniffing for treats. He was born without sections of his vertebrae, and therefore has inflammatory bowel disease and scoliosis, but that doesn't slow him down. He enjoys naps, cuddling, eating cucumbers, playing frisbee, and chasing his racquetball around the house. He is a registered Emotional Support Animal (ESA), and offers love to everyone who crosses his path.

Photos by @storytellersglobal